Kiviuq and the Mermaids

By Noel McDermott

Illustrated by Toma Feizo Gas

INHABIT
MEDIA

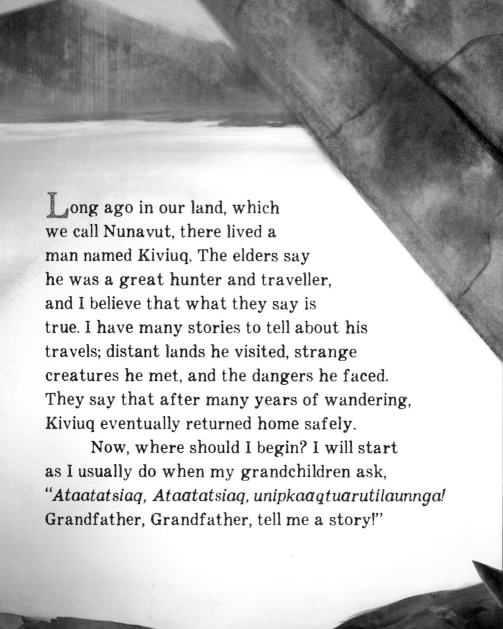

Long ago in our land, which
we call Nunavut, there lived a
man named Kiviuq. The elders say
he was a great hunter and traveller,
and I believe that what they say is
true. I have many stories to tell about his
travels; distant lands he visited, strange
creatures he met, and the dangers he faced.
They say that after many years of wandering,
Kiviuq eventually returned home safely.

Now, where should I begin? I will start
as I usually do when my grandchildren ask,
"*Ataatatsiaq, Ataatatsiaq, unipkaaqtuarutilaunnga!*
Grandfather, Grandfather, tell me a story!"

One day in spring, Kiviuq was at sea in his *qajaq* when he heard several hunters shouting. "*Natsiq, natsiq,* a seal, a seal," they called. All the hunters, including Kiviuq, began chasing the lone seal, which swam farther and farther out to sea.

The wind was getting stronger and the waves were growing bigger. But all the hunters kept following the seal.

Suddenly the seal began to chant an *irinaliuti*, a magic song, asking the wind and waves to help him: "*Silaga nauk?* Where is my weather? *Silaga nauk?* Where is my weather?" Kiviuq knew that song. He had often heard an old woman at his camp singing it to her grandson. Inuit said she was a shaman, an *angakkuq*, and that she had magic power with which she could control the weather. Kiviuq knew then that this was no ordinary seal.

Before long, the wind was roaring like an angry walrus and the waves were higher than an iceberg. Kiviuq struggled to keep his qajaq upright, and many times he thought he was going to drown.

As he was tossed by the waves, the spirits of the sea bird *saurraq* and *nanuq* the polar bear came to help Kiviuq. Nanuq beat back the wind and saurraq guided his qajaq into calm water. The elders say that Inuit only get help from the spirits when they really need it. So, once Kiviuq was safe, he had to rely on his own strength and experience to find his way home.

Kiviuq looked around, but there were no other hunters to be seen. He wondered why he was the only one who had survived the terrible storm.

It was then that Kiviuq realized that the seal must have been the grandson of the old angakkuq. The other hunters made fun of the boy for wearing his orphan rags and never allowed him to play games with the other children. His grandmother must have used her magic powers to change him into a seal to trick these unkind hunters. But Kiviuq never made fun of the boy, and he often gave meat to the boy's grandmother. Kiviuq was sure that was why he had been saved.

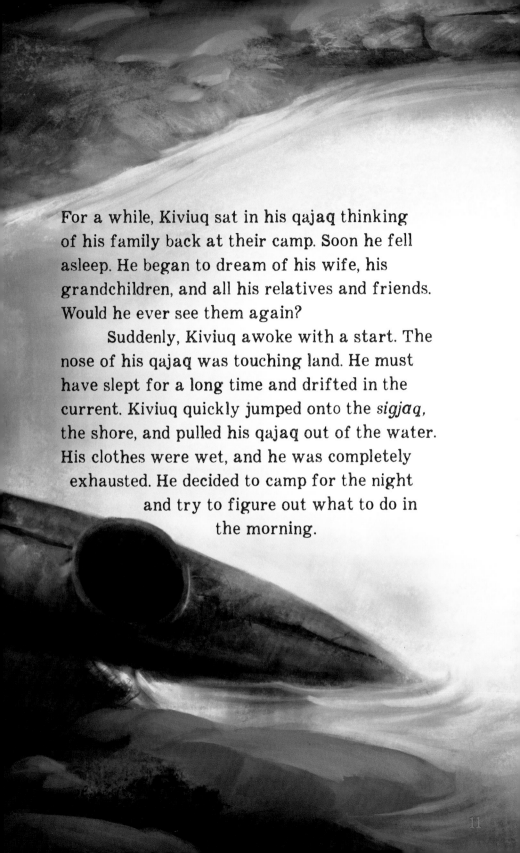

For a while, Kiviuq sat in his qajaq thinking
of his family back at their camp. Soon he fell
asleep. He began to dream of his wife, his
grandchildren, and all his relatives and friends.
Would he ever see them again?

Suddenly, Kiviuq awoke with a start. The
nose of his qajaq was touching land. He must
have slept for a long time and drifted in the
current. Kiviuq quickly jumped onto the *sigjaq,*
the shore, and pulled his qajaq out of the water.
His clothes were wet, and he was completely
exhausted. He decided to camp for the night
and try to figure out what to do in
the morning.

When he awoke, Kiviuq realized that he had landed on an island. There were plenty of seals to hunt, so he did not go hungry. The days passed quickly and Kiviuq began to regain his strength. He really missed his family. It was already fall and ice was beginning to form on the sea. If he didn't leave the island soon, he would be stuck there for the entire winter.

So, Kiviuq packed food and water in a sealskin bag, stored it inside his qajaq, and set off.

As he scanned the horizon, wondering which way to go, Kiviuq noticed something moving in the water. It looked like an *ugjuq,* a bearded seal. Kiviuq got his harpoon ready in case the ugjuq should attack his qajaq. As it swam closer, Kiviuq was surprised to see that it was actually a young *tuutalik,* a mermaid.

Now, it is not every day that one sees a tuutalik. But Kiviuq knew that he had to be careful. The elders say that *tuutaliit* may try to trick a person. They pretend to be friendly, but when they get close they can turn nasty.

The mermaid swam up close to Kiviuq's qajaq, and then she suddenly dived beneath the water. Kiviuq looked into the sea where she had disappeared, but he couldn't see her.

Then Kiviuq heard a voice from behind him calling, "Why don't you try to catch me."

Kiviuq turned and saw the tuutalik floating just beyond the end of his qajaq, smiling at him.

She called out as she had before, "Why don't you try to catch me."

Before Kiviuq could say a word, with a flip of her tail, she disappeared under the waves. But before long, she was back.

This time the tuutalik came up right in front
of the qajaq. Kiviuq could see her blue eyes and
smell the seaweed in her long, black hair. She
had human hands with long, sharp fingernails.
She was not smiling now.

In a loud voice she cried, "If you do not try
to catch me, I will rip your qajaq to pieces."

She began to tear at the seams in the
sealskin cover of the qajaq. Kiviuq shouted to
her to stop, but she ignored him. Kiviuq paddled
quickly backwards to shake her off. He looked
around, but the mermaid was gone.

Kiviuq decided to get away from there
as fast as he could. But suddenly there she was
again, scratching and tearing at the qajaq with
her nails.

Kiviuq swung his qajaq around in a circle, trying to avoid the mermaid. But no matter how fast he went, the tuutalik quickly caught up with him. She was a very powerful swimmer. She grabbed the front of the qajaq and shoved it down into the water. She kept repeating the same thing, "If you do not try to catch me, I will tear your qajaq to pieces."

Each time the front of the qajaq went under the water, Kiviuq got soaked with frigid seawater. He was sure he was going to be dumped into the sea. Kiviuq thought he was going to drown, so he decided to take action.

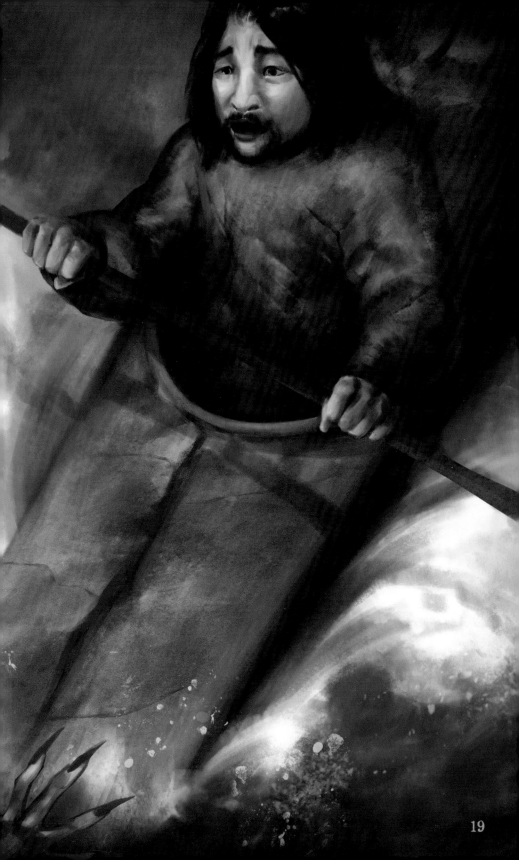

The qajaq was moving all over the place, up and down, and side to side. The saltwater splashed into Kiviuq's eyes. He grabbed his *unaaq*, his harpoon, and tried to push the mermaid away from the boat, but she dodged out of the way. Again Kiviuq tried, and again the tuutalik got out of the way. Finally, Kiviuq hit the mermaid on the head. She let out a loud cry and let go of the qajaq.

Before Kiviuq could paddle away, she caught the end of the harpoon and held on tight. That's when Kiviuq learned that mermaids are very strong. Back and forth they struggled for a long time. At last the tuutalik got tired and let go of the unaaq.

She glared at Kiviuq and in a loud voice cried, "You will not get away!"

She quickly moved away from the qajaq and dived deep down into the sea. Kiviuq noticed that she held one hand to her head as she swam.

Kiviuq paddled furiously for some distance,
but he was so tired after his fight with the
mermaid that he soon gave up and let his qajaq
drift on the waves. He fell asleep, but very
quickly was awakened by loud shouting and
screaming. Kiviuq didn't know where he was. He
looked around, and what he saw terrified him.
The sea was full of tuutaliit. But these creatures
were much bigger than the first tuutalik he
had encountered. Huge, muscular, and scaly, the
beasts splashed, jumped, and dived all around
him. The young tuutalik had brought her

relatives to help keep her promise that Kiviuq would never get away. They looked very, very angry.

Without hesitation, they raced right up to Kiviuq and began to scratch and tear at the skin of his qajaq. One smashed its tail against the side of the boat. The blow was so hard that Kiviuq almost fell into the water. Another jumped right out of the water and grabbed his paddle. It tried to pull the paddle from Kiviuq. It tugged and pulled, but Kiviuq held on and would not let go. With a mighty push of his paddle Kiviuq knocked the tuutalik back into the water.

Kiviuq knew that he had no chance against
so many tuutaliit. They would soon rip open
his qajaq. He tried to fight them off with his
harpoon, but it was useless. He had to make it
to land. The tuutaliit, creatures of the sea, could
not follow him there.

The mermaids surrounded Kiviuq,
screaming and shouting. He could see their long
nails trying to rip holes in his qajaq. The water
was white with foam. Kiviuq gathered all the
strength left in his body, plunged his paddle
into the water, and burst past them going as
fast as he could. He did not look back, but he
knew the mermaids were not far behind.

The mermaids were gaining on Kiviuq when he spotted some floating ice connected to a small island. This was his one chance. Some of the mermaids were getting very close. One of them caught the end of the qajaq with the tips of its nails just as Kiviuq leapt onto the ice. Kiviuq quickly pulled the qajaq up after him.

He just made it.

But the mermaids were not finished yet. Some of them dived under the ice. Their angry faces glared at Kiviuq from below. He could hear the scratching of their nails on the ice. He was afraid they would get ahead of him and break through the ice before he could get to the land. Kiviuq ran as fast as he could, trailing his qajaq behind him.

Kiviuq's legs felt like two blocks of ice and he could hardly catch his breath. He could go no farther. He stopped just where the ice met the land, and that's where the mermaids gave up the chase. They thrashed about in the water, moving in a large circle. Then, with one loud, angry shout, together they all swam out to the deep water and dived out of sight.

For a long time, Kiviuq could not move. He stood on the sigjaq looking out to sea. There was no movement on the water. It was as calm as a sheet of ice. Kiviuq realized that the mermaids were finally gone. He never wanted to see another tuutalik ever again.

Kiviuq pulled his qajaq up onto the land to make sure it would not float away on the tide. He turned it upside down to empty out the seawater. There were scratches and tears on the front of the qajaq, and one large hole at the back, but Kiviuq knew he could repair the damage. He set up his little tent, gathered moss and sticks to make a fire, and cooked some seal meat.

After Kiviuq had eaten, he took a walk along the sigjaq, just to make sure there were no tuutaliit about.

Back in his tent, Kiviuq got into his caribou-skin sleeping bag and drifted into sleep. He didn't sleep very well that night because he had bad dreams.

What do you think he dreamt about?

That's all I can remember, for now: *taima*.

Glossary of Inuktitut terms

angakkuq
(pronounced "an-ga-kook") — shaman

ataatatsiaq
(pronounced "a-taa-tat-see-ak") — Grandfather

irinaliuti
(pronounced "er-e-na-lee-oo-te") — a magic song or chant

Kiviuq
(pronounced "key-ve-ook") — name of a great traveller from Inuit traditional stories.

nanuq
(pronounced "na-nook") — polar bear

natsiq
(pronounced "nat-sek") — seal

qajaq
(pronounced "ka-yak") — kayak, a one-man boat

saurraq
(pronounced "saw-oo-raak") —phalarope, a type of seabird

sigjaq
(pronounced "seg-jack") — the shore

Silaga nauk?
(pronounced "see-la-ga na-uk?") —phrase meaning "Where is my weather?"

taima
(pronounced "ta-ee-ma") — the end

tuutaliit
(pronounced "too-ta-leet") — many mermaids

tuutalik
(pronounced "too-ta-lik") — a mermaid

ugjuq
(pronounced "og-jok ") — bearded seal

unaaq
(pronounced "oo-naak") — harpoon

unipkaaqtuarutilaunnga
(pronounced "oo-nip-kaak-two-a-ro-tee-law-oo-nn-ga") —
word meaning "tell me a story"

Contributors

Noel McDermott

Noel McDermott is a retired professor of literature at Nunavut Arctic College in Iqaluit, Nunavut, where he lived and taught in Inuktitut and English for thirty-five years as a classroom teacher, school principal, and lecturer in the teacher training program. He has held teaching appointments at many other educational institutions, including McGill University, Trent University, and the University of Waterloo, as well as at the Sami University in Kautokeino, Norway. He has taught introductory Inuktitut and Inuit history at Queen's University for the past four years. His previous book was *Akinirmut Unipkaaqtuat: Stories of Revenge*.

Toma Feizo Gas

From his early days of reading sci-fi and fantasy books, Toma has been fascinated with the dramatic scenes portrayed on the covers of those books. There started his lifelong love affair with telling stories through pictures. Today, Toma's key influence remains the people in these stories, the motives that drive us, and the decisions that shape us, propelling him to craft bold visual statements and contrast in his own art. As a career illustrator, his work can be found gracing the pages and covers of titles such as *Dungeons & Dragons*, *Pathfinder*, the *Star Wars* and *Mutant Chronicles* role playing games, as well as several upcoming fantasy novel series.

Published by Inhabit Media Inc. • www.inhabitmedia.com

Inhabit Media Inc. (Iqaluit), P.O. Box 11125, Iqaluit, Nunavut, X0A 1H0
(Toronto), 191 Eglinton Avenue East, Suite 301, Toronto, Ontario, M4P 1K1

Editors: Neil Christopher and Louise Flaherty
Art director: Danny Christopher

We acknowledge the financial support of the Government of Canada through the
Department of Canadian Heritage Canada Book Fund.

We acknowledge the support of the Canada Council for the Arts for our publishing
program.

ISBN: 978-1-77227-082-2
Printed in Canada

| Canadian Patrimoine | Canada Council | Conseil des Arts |
| Heritage canadien | for the Arts | du Canada |

Library and Archives Canada Cataloguing in Publication

McDermott, Noel, author
        Kiviuq and the mermaids / by Noel McDermott ; illustrated
by Toma Feizo Gas.

ISBN 978-1-77227-082-2 (hardback)

        1. Kiviuq (Legendary character)--Juvenile fiction. 2. Mermaids--
Juvenile fiction. I. Gas, Toma Feizo, illustrator II. Title.

PS8625.D44K59 2016   jC813'.6   C2016-903078-4

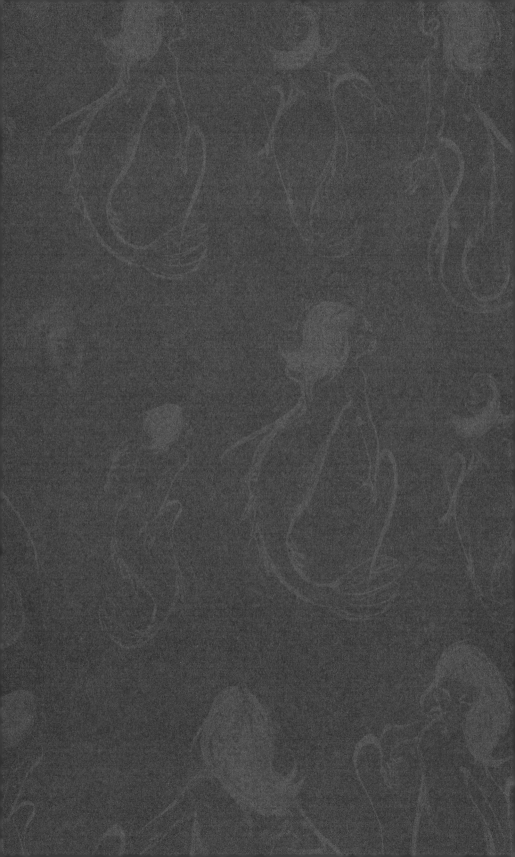